THE OLD PIRATE
OF CENTRAL PARK

✎ ROBERT PRIEST ✎

HOUGHTON MIFFLIN COMPANY

BOSTON

FOR COURTLAND

The text of this book is set in Janson.
The illustrations are airbrushed enamel on clayboard.

Library of Congress Cataloging-in-Publication Data

Priest, Robert, 1951–
The old pirate of Central Park / written and illustrated by Robert Priest.
p.   cm.
Summary: A retired pirate and a retired queen engage in a thunderous
battle to gain control of the Central Park sailboat pond.
HC ISBN-13: 978-0-395-90505-0   PA ISBN-13: 978-0-618-99769-5
[1. Pirates—Fiction. 2. Kings, queens, rulers, etc.—Fiction.
3. Sailboats—Fiction. 4. Central Park (New York, N.Y.)—Fiction.
5. New York, N.Y.—Fiction.]   I. Title
PZ7.P9342901   1999
[Fic]—dc21   98-11913 CIP AC

Printed in Malaysia
TWP 10 9 8 7 6 5 4 3

In a tall ornate New York City apartment building, there lives an old retired Pirate.

One morning, while walking in Central Park, the Old Pirate started remembering his life as the swashbuckling captain of the notorious pirate ship *The Laughing Dog*.

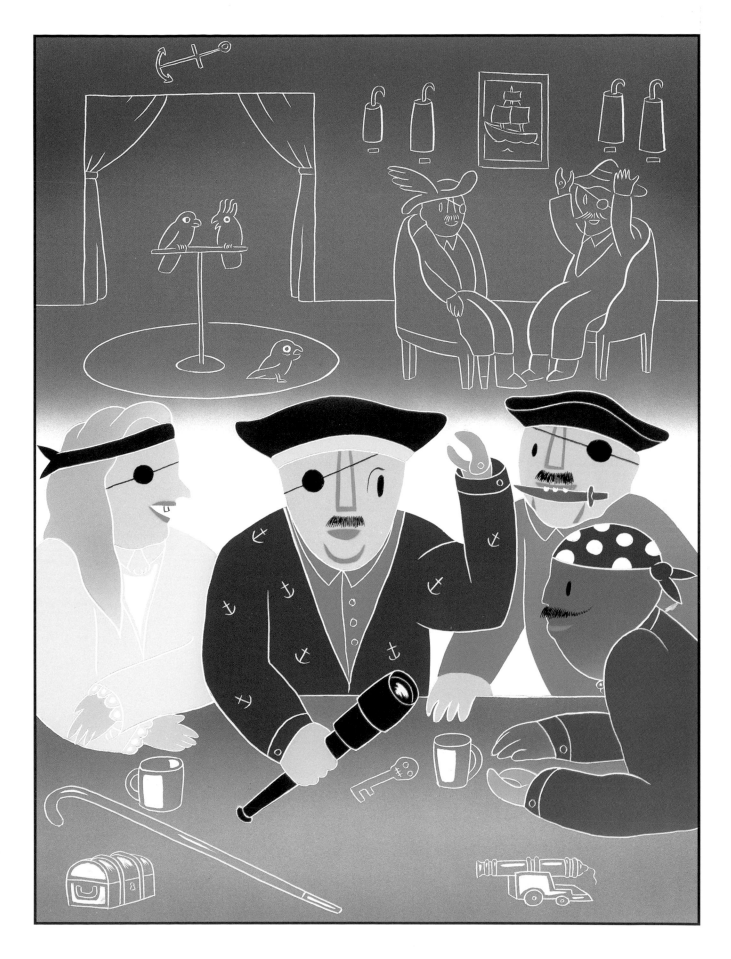

That afternoon, at the Old Pirates' Club, he told his friends about it.

And that evening, with his tools scattered about, he sat at his kitchen table and began to build.

"What are you up to?" asked his little green parrot.
"You'll see, matey" was the Old Pirate's mysterious reply.

Day after day he measured and fitted. Slowly a little wooden vessel began to take shape in the apartment, high above Central Park.

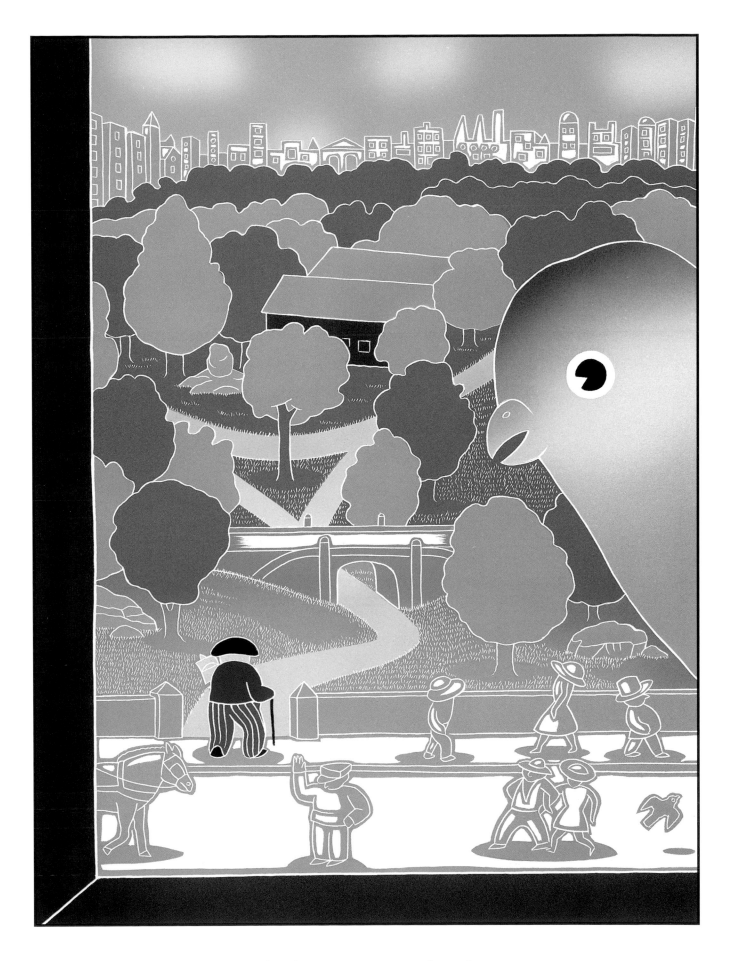

Finally one morning, the boat was completed.
He picked up his new ship and hurried into the Park.

Soon the Old Pirate arrived at the Central Park Sailboat Pond, where a splendid fleet of model boats tacked to and fro.

Children's laughter filled the air as schooners, yachts, and frigates of every color, shape, and size gracefully skimmed the peaceful blue waters of the lagoon.

The Old Pirate launched his vessel and inspected her. She was a perfect replica of his old ship, *The Laughing Dog*.

"Shiver me timbers," he cried, "it's good to be on the water again."

Just then a retired Queen, all decked out in jewels, showed up at the pond.

The Queen had her Butler, Jeeves, launch her ship, the S.S. *Uppity Duchess*, which commenced with utter, reckless, and heedless abandon to race pell-mell around the pond.

It swamped sloops, dunked dories, and drenched dinghies.

Even *The Laughing Dog* was nearly sunk.

"Your majesty," cried the Old Pirate. "Slow down and share the seas."

"How dare that pesky Old Pirate give *me* an order! Jeeves," cried the Queen, "reprimand that impertinent scalawag!"

Suddenly, with a bang, a miniature cannon fired a miniature cannon-ball from the deck of the *Uppity Duchess*. It bounced off the foredeck of *The Laughing Dog*, severely testing the little ship's seaworthiness.

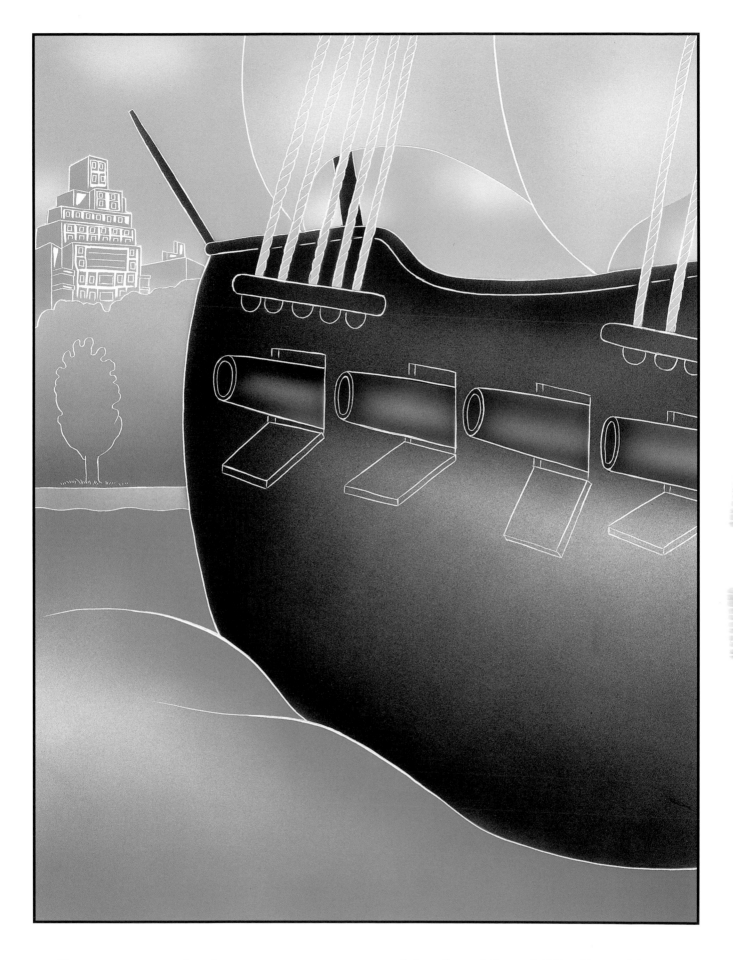

In response, six tiny cannons appeared in the side of *The Laughing Dog* and fired.

Thus began the infamous Battle of Central Park.

Smoke filled the air as tiny cannonballs flew everywhere.

People hid under tables and wondered if someone was making a movie.

Dogs broke free and ran wild after years of being cooped up in tiny apartments.

Even the bravest cabbies dared not continue down Fifth Avenue.

Children ran this way and that, collecting the little cannonballs.

The thunder of the battle reached a crescendo that could be heard
all the way to Harlem.

And then all went quiet, an eerie quiet never before heard in New York City. Out of the smoke appeared Jeeves, carrying a message from the Queen.

It read . . .

Mr. Pirate,
I am late for my
afternoon nap. Therefore
I request a truce and
will herefore and forevermore
agree to share the seas.
Her Royal Highness,
THE QUEEN

The Old Pirate needed a nap, too, so he and the Queen shook hands
and agreed to a truce . . .

and peace and tranquility once again reigned at the pond.

Sails were set, dogs recaptured, and gentle laughter returned to the soft summer air of New York City.

It turned out that ships, treasures, and high diplomacy were just a few of the interests shared by the Old Pirate and the Old Queen. Today one can find them sitting together on a bench beside the pond, two happy peas in a pod, the two "Old Retirates" of Central Park.